The Singing Bones

Inspired by Grimms' Fairy Tales

shaun tan

FOREWORD BY NEIL GAIMAN
INTRODUCED BY JACK ZIPES

ARTHUR A. LEVINE BOOKS
AN IMPRINT OF SCHOLASTIC INC.

For Vida

CONTENTS

FOREWORD

Neil Gaiman

There are stories, honed by the retelling, simplified by the people who recorded them and transmitted them, old stories, with the edges rubbed off them, like the pebbles on a beach, each story the perfect size and heft to send skimming over the water, or to use to strike an enemy.

Folktales are like jokes: If they had a beginning, it is lost to us. They wander in and out of style, in and out of history, as they are told in pubs and in bedrooms, in fields and around campfires.

The Brothers Grimm collected these folktales and fairy tales. They recorded them, rewrote them, reworked them on occasion, sanitized them, and never knew that their life's work, the thing by which they would be remembered, would not be the hefty volumes of German grammar and philology that they loved, but the stories collected for them by their friends and family, told by laborers and grandmothers, that they would publish for adults and which would find currency with children.

The stories that the Grimms collected were no more the real tales than a joke in a joke book is the same joke that would be told, with asides and details and interjections, by a raconteur to a willing audience in a town tavern. They are plans, schematics, reminders.

People need stories. It's one of the things that make us who we are. We crave stories, because they make us more than ourselves, they give us escape and they give us knowledge. They entertain us and they change us, as they have changed and entertained us for thousands of years.

Grimms' stories have been illustrated before (obviously; unillustrated versions are rare) but they have never been illustrated like this.

These are photographs of sculptures that each summon, or perhaps evoke, a specific tale from the Grimm Brothers' canon. They were made by an artist and writer named Shaun Tan.

I first met Shaun about twenty years ago at a science-fiction convention in Perth, but I only half-remember meeting him. He's quiet and shy. I got to know him slightly better with each subsequent trip to Australia, and Shaun got used to me introducing myself to him. He would always point out that actually we'd already met. He's an artist and a writer and a film director, a person with a peculiar and singular vision. He creates stories, sometimes wordless, always told with economy, which manage to be both alienating and welcoming. They make you feel, somehow, like you are a stranger and also that you have found your place, that you belong.

Shaun Tan lives in Melbourne. He has an easy smile when he relaxes. He does not seem to mind that I only spell his first name right half the time.

My son is three months old. He looks out with wide blue eyes, but he experiences the world as much through his mouth as anything: His mouth is his eyes, and that which can be put into his mouth is being seen as much as it is being tasted. I had forgotten that this was so, but having small children around brings back memories of what it was like to discover the universe by mouth: of the salty feel of a pebble on the beach, or the bone or plastic hardness of a button.

There is a tactile quality to the Shaun Tan sculptures. They feel primal, as if they were made in a long-ago age of the world, when the stories were first being shaped, and that perhaps the sculptures came first.

In these pictures, we find wit and imagination. We observe the stunning way Shaun uses, and does not use, color. But above all there is the tactility. I want to hold these sculptures, to pick them up. I want to squeeze them in my hands as I walk in the dark, to put them into my pockets and feel them there, reassuring me.

The heroes, villains, heroines, animals, children, of Grimms' stories are not individuals. They are barely people. They have no existence before the story begins, and no life afterward. They are types, simply drawn, with only the details that you need to know in order for the story to work: This one is brave, that one is beautiful, this one is too foolish to know fear, that one killed his previous wives, this one will pick nettles in a graveyard at midnight to save her brothers from their curse.

Which means, in a strange way, that any specific depiction of them must be wrong.

A drawing of a princess more beautiful than the dawn will not show us the princess conjured up in our mind's eye. The great fairy-tale artists of the last two centuries gave us personal depictions — Edmund Dulac's colorful palaces, for example; Kay Nielsen's skies and animals; Arthur Rackham's gnarled and grasping trees — but each of them drew figures who were specific people, ways of seeing the world that were more complex, perhaps more beautiful, than the tales they were illustrating.

Shaun Tan does something else here: something profound. His sculptures suggest, they do not describe. They imply, they do not delineate. They are, in themselves, stories: not the frozen moments in time that a classical illustration needs to be. These are something new, something deeper. They do not look like moments of the stories: instead, they feel like the stories themselves.

In this book are photographs of simple, touchable shapes that somehow contain worlds. The images are not literal. Instead they are dizzyingly oneiric: Size is relative, shapes are mutable (look at the witch, towering over the candy cottage, as Hansel and Gretel eat their fill; see the tower that is also Rapunzel, for it has a face and long, long hair). They can be as gray and abstract as the statues, winged and armless, of "The Maiden Without Hands"; as colorful as the every-fruit tree in which skeletal Death waits in "Gambling Hans"; as nightmarish as the laughing creature who symbolizes Rumpelstiltskin; as haunting and as vulnerable as the delicate leg stepping from the fur covering that protects and hides the heroine in "All Fur."

Here they gather for you, timeless and perfect, a mixture of darkness and light that manages to capture Grimms' stories in a way that nobody, to my knowledge, has done before.

Shaun Tan makes me want to hold these tales close, to rub them with my fingers, to feel the cracks and the creases and the edges of them. He makes me want to pick them up, inspect them from unusual angles, feel the heft and the weight of them. He makes me wonder what damage I could do with them, how badly I could hurt someone if I hit them with a story.

These pictures make me want to put the stories into my mouth, knowing that I will eventually have to spit them out again, reluctantly, in words.

HOW THE BROTHERS GRIMM MADE THEIR WAY INTO THE WORLD

Jack Zipes

How is it possible for two country lads named Jacob and Wilhelm Grimm, born in the provincial German town of Hanau in 1785 and 1786, to have become world famous simply by collecting folk and fairy tales? If they were alive today, they would probably be surprised to learn that the seventh final edition of their tales published in 1857 has been translated into one hundred and sixty languages and cultural dialects and that UNESCO officially inscribed their collection of tales, *Kinder- und Hausmärchen* (*Children's and Household Tales*), in the *Memory of the World Register* in 2005. Yet, they believed that their voluminous philological studies were more important than their revised collections of tales. So, what would they say to the numerous bicentenary celebrations of their first edition of 1812/1815 that took place all over the world from 2012 to 2015?

There's a tale to be told here, somewhat like the one they collected, "How Six Made Their Way in the World," about a discharged and disgruntled soldier, who is poorly paid and mistreated by a brutal king and goes off to unite with five superheroes to gain revenge if not justice. In the Grimms' case, however, the "fairy tale" about their lives involves a traumatic loss of social status and personal suffering after their father, a well-to-do and respected magistrate, unexpectedly died in 1796. It involves setting out into the world with fortitude and pulling yourself up by your bootstraps — with a dose of rebellion against kings.

So, once there was this widow, who had five sons and a daughter, and was beside herself after her husband had died in 1796 because she had very little money and no real means to support herself and her large family. Fortunately, her father and relatives helped her for a while so that she could send her two eldest sons, Jacob and Wilhelm, eleven and ten years of age, to an elite school in Kassel, a major city in Hesse. Socially disadvantaged, the brothers knew that they had to prove themselves in their studies, and both became valedictorians and went on to study law at the University of Marburg in 1802 and 1803. But it was not law that eventually interested them. Rather, it was philology. The Grimms came to believe that ancient texts, sagas, epics, legends, myths, animal stories, and wonder tales contained essential truths about rituals, traditions, and living conditions in central and northern Europe. They felt that the study of folklore was a means to pass on a rich common heritage to the German people, and so the brothers made a solemn vow to work together for the rest of their lives to uncover and preserve the gems of ancient literature and customs. Spoken and written words were holy for the Grimms, and they felt they could enable the disunited German people to create bonds through stories that would unify them and develop a more just nation-state.

The vow they made to each other was recorded during revolutionary times in Europe. It was a period when German classical and romantic literature flourished. Writers such as Goethe, Schiller, Novalis, Tieck, Eichendorff, Brentano, Achim von Arnim, E. T. A. Hoffmann, and others produced major works. Beethoven, Glück, and other composers stunned the world of music. Experimentation was the rule in all cultural and economic fields. But the Napoleonic Wars that followed the French Revolution were also rampant at the beginning of the nineteenth century, and the city of Kassel was invaded and occupied by the French. The Grimms experienced another shock when their mother died in 1808, and they became responsible for the welfare of their three brothers and sister. So they lived frugally and worked hard. Jacob became a diplomat for a while, and Wilhelm a librarian. Meanwhile, they kept collecting manuscripts, texts, books, and tales, and writing essays and books about medieval songs, poems, and stories. By 1812, after collecting about ninety tales for their friend Clemens Brentano, who discarded them, the Grimms took them and published them in the first volume of *Children's and Household Tales*, with a scholarly preface and notes, and this volume was followed by a second one in 1815.

To their disappointment, these two volumes that constituted the first edition were not well received. Critics and friends found the collection too scholarly, somewhat offensive, bleak, colorless, loaded with footnotes, and without illustrations. But the Grimms would not abandon their project. They had faith in the relevance of the tales. By 1816 both were librarians in Kassel. Wilhelm took charge of editing the second edition of *Children's and Household Tales* while together they produced a two-volume collection of *German Legends*, and Jacob wrote a massive study of *German Grammar*. When, in 1819, the second edition of their tales also received severe criticism, despite the fact that Wilhelm had made many changes, they resolutely kept collecting tales and even translating Irish and Scandinavian tales. Then, out of the blue, a package arrived that was to change the destiny of their tales.

In 1823 they received a copy of the first English translation of part of the tales in their 1819 edition, published under the title *German Popular Stories*. It was sent from London by the translator, Edgar Taylor, who was a lawyer and folklorist. Art and translations of their tales were far from the minds of the assiduous brothers, more concerned with recuperating ancient stories connected to the German cultural heritage than having their tales illustrated and disseminated in other countries; that is, until *German Popular Stories* arrived. This sparkling edition contained eleven illustrations by the brilliant caricaturist George Cruikshank, who added nine more in 1826, and they were so unusual and entertaining that the Grimms, who wanted their work to be better known by the German reading public, decided to create a special family edition of their tales in 1825 that included seven "gothic" copper engravings by their brother Ludwig. These were later replaced by Ludwig Pietsch's boring but cute black-and-white lithographs. This so-called "small edition" of fifty tales was printed ten times through 1858 with various illustrations during the Grimms' lifetime, and it ran more or less parallel with the "large edition," which continued to include prefaces and notes, and was published seven times with revisions and culminated with two hundred and ten tales in 1857 without illustrations.

So, ironically, the Grimms, who had sought to make their mark primarily as serious philologists, were now destined to become popular and famous because readers began interpreting their sanitized and censored editions published after the third 1837 edition and all the small editions as books for children. Glad that the reception of their tales had become more positive, the brothers continued to focus their energies more on developing their academic career. Indeed, they had become so well respected because of their philological publications that they could leave Kassel in 1829 to accept professorships in philology at the renowned University of Göttingen. By this time Wilhelm had married Dorothea Wild, one of the best contributors of stories to the first edition; Jacob, who never married, continued to live with Wilhelm and his family, their desks always facing each other, their vow intact.

The Grimms were greatly admired in Göttingen, where they wrote and published books about German linguistics, law, and customs. However, given their liberal politics, they were banished by the King of Hanover in 1837 because they refused to take an oath of loyalty to him that would have broken the constitution and made the king an absolute dictator. They literally fled for their lives to Kassel, where they continued to work on proverbs and began writing the enormous *German Dictionary*, the first of its kind in German-speaking regions. They now had no salaries and had to live from commissions. Fortunately, in 1840, they both received offers to teach at the Humboldt University in Berlin, where they spent the rest of their lives. While Wilhelm was in charge of all the revised editions of *Children's and Household Tales*, both he and Jacob devoted most of their attention to editing the *German Dictionary* as well as writing essays and books on the history of the German language and folklore. At the same time they showed strong support for the causes of the 1848 revolution in Germany, and Jacob traveled to Frankfurt am Main to represent Berlin and was given a place of honor in the general assembly.

The Grimms never stopped collecting and writing even after both retired from the university by 1852. They never sought fame and never thought that the tales they collected would be revered throughout the world. The country lads died humbly and peacefully, Wilhelm in 1859 and Jacob in 1863.

But this is not the end of my story, or rather, not the end of the "fairy tale" about the Grimms and their collection of folk and fairy tales. Without the help of modern technology and the mass media, their tales, which they regarded as divinely inspired stories of ordinary people, began spreading throughout Europe, North America, and the rest of the world. In addition, whether in large editions, toy and chapbooks, broadsides, or single picture books, the tales were generally illustrated. Though the early illustrations were more decorative and comic than interpretative and serious, they led to a flourishing of unusual illustrations by the turn of the twentieth century. I am thinking here of British, German, French, Czech, Scandinavian, and American illustrators — Richard Doyle, Walter Crane, Edward Wehnert, Arthur Rackham, Albert Weisgerber, Edmund Dulac, Jennie Harbour, Jessie Willcox Smith, Otto Ubbelohde, Johnny Gruelle, Kay Nielsen, Jiří Trnka, Josef Scharl, Gustaf Tenggren, and Fritz Kredel up through Wanda Gág. Their imaginative and diverse approaches to the Grimms' tales enriched and embellished them, but they all tended to minimize the brutal human struggles in the majority of the tales because the Grimms' original target audience had changed from adults to children in the course of the nineteenth century. And it should be noted that it was a change promoted largely by publishers.

It was not until the rise of the feminist movement in the 1970s that innovations in illustration and adaptation of the Grimms' tales by such major writers as Anne Sexton, Angela Carter, Tanith Lee, and Margaret Atwood began to take place. Critical illustrations of the Grimms' tales can be seen in the work of Maurice Sendak and David Hockney, but the most explosive interpretive illustrations have been done in the twenty-first century by Nikolaus Heidelbach and Susanne Janssen in Germany, Fabian Negrin in Italy, and Andrea Dezsö in America, not to mention the paintings and sculptures of Kiki Smith, Paula Rego, Sharon Singer,

Gina Litherland, Natalie Frank, and other experimental artists. Their depictions of the Grimms' tales are unsettling, and challenge readers and viewers to question the texts and the feelings they arouse. These artists dig deep into the stories and stamp the tales with their own personal and peculiar visions. They do not simply represent key scenes. They do not decorate. They interpret and deepen the narratives visually by shocking conventional perspectives.

Meanwhile, another "country lad" by the name of Shaun Tan has made his way into the cosmopolitan world of European and American art from lively Perth, Australia, to engage himself with the Grimms' tales, not to shock and challenge but to explore and mold the Grimms' tales in a way that, I believe, would have met with their approval. In many respects, the Grimms' tales, which were not their own but were more like found objects that might have died without the Grimms' creative and sensitive touch, have been given new life by Tan's highly unusual sculptures. By re-creating the figures of the tales, the animals and humans, as solid miniatures in contrasting colors, Tan has generated a rediscovery of the Grimms' tales and tells them visually anew: The tales found by the Grimms are to be found once again by readers and viewers of Tan's stunning sculptures.

Underlying his artwork is the principle of estrangement. In Tan's rendition of "How Six Made Their Way in the World," the heroes are most unheroic-looking. They stand in a semicircle on what seems to be a chessboard. They are not placed in exact positions. It doesn't seem as if they will move off into the world. Yet they are eccentric and extraordinary, and these little figures will soon do wonders in the world. Little people can be empowered through art.

All Tan's sculptures estrange us and beckon us to gaze and think about moving them, to discover how they have been made, and why they have been drawn from the Grimms' tales. They have been taken out of one world and installed in another setting. This is what the Grimms did with the tales they collected, and there is something like an elective affinity between Tan and the Brothers Grimm. Or perhaps I should say "electrical" affinity, because Tan has transformed the Grimms' tales into miraculous artworks that will move and speak for themselves.

RECOMMENDED READING

Briggs, Katharine M. "The Influence of the Brothers Grimm in England." In *Brüder Grimm Gedenken*. Ed. Ludwig Denecke and Ina-Maria Greverus. Vol. 1 Marburg: N. G. Elwert, 1963. 511–24.

Bown, Nicola. *Fairies in Nineteenth-Century Art and Literature*. Cambridge: Cambridge University Press, 2001.

Haase, Donald, ed. *The Reception of Grimms' Fairy Tales: Reponses, Reactions, Revisions*. Detroit: Wayne State University Press, 1993.

_____. "Re-Viewing the Grimm Corpus: Grimm Scholarship in an Era of Celebrations." *Monatshefte* 91 (1999): 121–31.

_____. "Framing the Brothers Grimm: Paratexts and Intercultural Transmission in Postwar English-Language Editions of the *Kinder- und Hausmärchen*." *Fabula* 44.1/2 (2003): 55–69.

Joosen, Vanessa and Gillian Lathey, eds. *Grimms' Tales Around the Globe: The Dynamics of Their International Reception*. Detroit: Wayne State University Press, 2014.

Kamenetsky, Christa. *The Brothers Grimm and Their Critics: Folktales and the Quest for Meaning*. Athens, OH: Ohio University Press, 1992.

Neumann, Siegfried. "The Brothers Grimm as Collectors and Editors of German Folktales." *The Reception of Grimms' Fairy Tales: Response, Reactions, Revisions*. Ed. Donald Haase. Detroit: Wayne State University Press, 1993. 24–40.

Paradiž, Valerie. *Clever Maids: The Secret History of the Grimm Fairy Tales*. New York: Basic Books, 2005.

Patten, Robert. "George Cruikshank's Grimm Humor." In Joachim Müller, ed. *Imagination on a Long Rein: English Literature Illustrated*. Marburg: Jonas, 1988. 13–28.

_____. *George Cruikshank: Life, Times, and Art*. 2 vols. New Brunswick, NJ: Rutgers University Press, 1992.

Robinson, Orrin W. *Grimm Language: Grammar, Gender, and Genuineness in the Fairy Tales*. Amsterdam: John Benjamins, 2010.

Schacker, Jennifer. *National Dreams: The Remaking of Fairy Tales in Nineteenth-Century England*. Philadelphia: University of Pennsylvania Press, 2003.

Sutton, Martin. *The Sin-Complex: A Critical Study of English Versions of the Grimms' Kinder- und Hausmärchen in the Nineteenth Century*. Kassel: Schriften der Brüder Grimm-Gesellschaft, 1996.

Tatar, Maria. *The Hard Facts of the Grimms' Fairy Tales*. Princeton: Princeton University Press, 1987.

Zipes, Jack. *The Brothers Grimm: From Enchanted Forests to the Modern World* (1988). rev. and expanded 2nd ed. New York: Palgrave, 2002.

_____. *Grimm Legacies: The Magical Power of the Grimms' Folk and Fairy Tales*. Princeton: Princeton University Press, 2014.

_____, ed. *The Oxford Companion to Fairy Tales*. 2nd rev. ed. Oxford: Oxford University Press, 2015.

PLATES

· I ·

THE FROG KING

"Oh yes," said the princess, "I'll promise you anything you want if only you'll bring back my precious golden ball from the bottom of the well!" However, she thought, What nonsense that stupid frog talks! He just sits in the water croaking with the rest of the frogs. How can he expect a human being to accept him as a companion?

THE COMPANIONSHIP OF
THE CAT AND THE MOUSE

When the cat and mouse arrived at the church where the pot of fat was kept, the mouse was shocked to find it empty. "Now I know what really happened when you went to be a godfather to all those kittens!" cried the mouse. "Some friend you turned out to be!"

"Don't you dare say another word," warned the cat.

"It was you who—"

Before the mouse could finish, the cat jumped on her and gobbled her up. That's just the way of the world.

HANSEL AND GRETEL

The roof was made of cake, and it tasted so good that Hansel ripped off a large piece and pulled it down, while Gretel pushed out a round piece of the sugar windowpane, sat, and ate it with great relish. Suddenly the door opened, and a very old woman leaning on a crutch came slinking out of the house. Hansel and Gretel were so tremendously frightened that they dropped what they had in their hands. But the old woman wagged her head and said, "Well now, dear children, who brought you here? Just come inside and stay with me. Nobody's going to harm you."

· 4 ·

LITTLE RED CAP

"Oh, Grandmother, what big ears you have!"

"The better to hear you with."

"Oh, Grandmother, what big hands you have!"

"The better to grab you with."

"Oh, Grandmother, what a terribly big mouth you have!"

"The better to eat you with!"

· 5 ·

THE BOY WHO LEFT HOME
TO FIND OUT ABOUT FEAR

The boy went to the gallows, sat down beneath it, and waited until
evening came. Since he was cold, he made a fire. When the wind
knocked the hanged men against one another and they swung back and
forth, he thought, They must be freezing up there, I'd better bring them
all down to sit by the fire. And so he did, one by one, all seven of them.
They sat there beside him without saying a word, without moving,
and soon enough their trousers caught on fire. "Be careful," he said,
"otherwise I'll hang you all back up there!"

6

FAITHFUL JOHANNES

"After my death, you're to show my son the entire castle," said the king, "all the rooms, halls, and vaults, along with the treasures that are in them. But never show him the room at the end of the long hallway, where the portrait of the Princess of the Golden Roof is hidden. If he sees that portrait, he'll fall passionately in love with her and be obliged to undertake great risks because of her. You must protect him against this."

7

THE TWELVE BROTHERS

Once upon a time a king and queen lived together peacefully and had twelve children, all boys. One day the king said to his wife, "When you give birth to our thirteenth child and it's a girl, the twelve boys must be put to death so she may have all the wealth and the kingdom for herself."

He even had twelve coffins made and filled with wood shavings. Each was fitted with a death pillow, and all the coffins were locked in a room. The king gave the key to the queen and ordered her never to say one word about this to anyone. She then sat and lamented the entire day, until her youngest son asked her, "Dear Mother, why are you so sad?"

8

THE WHITE SNAKE

The servant, while removing the king's dish, was overcome by curiosity. He took it into his room, and after he had carefully locked the door, he lifted the cover and found a white snake lying inside. Once he laid eyes on it, he had an irresistible desire to taste it. So he cut off a little piece and put it in his mouth. No sooner did his tongue touch it than he heard a strange whispering of exquisite voices outside his window. He went over to it to listen and noticed some sparrows talking to one another, telling what they had seen in the fields and forest. Tasting the snake had given him the power to understand the language of animals.

· 9 ·

LITTLE BROTHER
AND LITTLE SISTER

"Oh, brother!" the sister exclaimed. "Please don't drink from the spring, or you'll be turned into a deer and run away from me."

But the brother, who was already kneeling at the spring, leaned over and drank some of the water. Immediately after a few drops had touched his lips, he lay there in the form of a fawn. The sister began weeping over her poor bewitched brother, and the little fawn wept too.

Finally the girl said, "Hush, my dear little fawn. No matter what happens, I shall never forsake you."

· 10 ·

RAPUNZEL

Rapunzel grew to be the most beautiful child under the sun. But when she was twelve years old, the sorceress locked her in a tower that was in a forest. It had neither door nor stairs, only a little window high above. Whenever the sorceress wanted to visit her, she would stand below and call out, "Rapunzel, Rapunzel, let down your hair."

THE THREE LITTLE GNOMES IN THE FOREST

She thanked the little men by shaking hands with each of them and ran home to her stepmother, bringing the strawberries from the snow as had been demanded of her. As she entered the house and said, "Good evening," a piece of gold fell right out of her mouth. Then she explained what had happened to her in the forest, and with each word she uttered, gold pieces spilled from her mouth until soon the entire room was covered with gold.

"Just look at how arrogant she is!" her stepsister exclaimed. "The way she throws money around!"

But secretly the stepsister was envious and wanted to go into the forest and search for strawberries in the snow, so that she might also return with gold spilling from her lips.

12

THE THREE SNAKE LEAVES

The faithful servant had witnessed everything: how the young king's wife, consumed by passion for the ship's captain, murdered her poor husband and threw his body overboard. So the servant secretly unfastened a small boat and sailed after his master, fishing the dead man out of the sea as the traitors continued on their voyage. He put the magical snake leaves on his master's eyes and mouth and succeeded in bringing him back to life.

Now the two of them rowed day and night with all their might, and their little boat sailed so swiftly over the sea that they reached the old king before the others and told him everything that had happened. "I can't believe she would do such an awful thing," he said, "but the truth will soon come to light."

13

THE FISHERMAN
AND HIS WIFE

"Flounder, flounder, in the sea,
if you're a man, then speak to me.
Though I do not care for my wife's request,
I've come to ask it nonetheless."

"Well, what does she want?" asked the flounder.

"Oh, flounder," the man said, "my wife wants to be emperor."

"Go back home," said the flounder. "She's already emperor."

The fisherman went home, and when he arrived, the entire castle was made of polished marble and golden ornaments, surrounded by marching soldiers. Barons, counts, and dukes were inside the palace walking around like servants. They opened doors of pure gold for him, and as he entered, he saw his wife sitting on a two-mile-high throne made from a single piece of gold.

"Husband," she said, "why are you standing there? It's true that I'm emperor, but now I want to be pope. Go and tell this to the flounder."

14

THE BRAVE LITTLE TAILOR

The giant looked at the tailor contemptuously and said, "You crumb! You miserable creature!"

"Oh, you think so?" the little tailor responded, and opened his coat to show the giant his belt, embroidered with large letters. "You can read for yourself what kind of man I am!"

The giant read "Seven with one blow!" and thought that it meant the tailor had slain seven men, rather than the seven flies he had swatted in his workshop. Therefore, the giant began to show some respect for the little fellow.

15

CINDERELLA

They expected her to work hard from morning till night. She had to get up before dawn, carry water to the house, make the fire, cook, and wash. Moreover, her stepsisters did everything imaginable to cause her grief and make her look ridiculous. For instance, they poured peas and lentils into the hearth ashes so she had to sit there and pick them out. In the evening, when she was exhausted from working, they took away her bed, and she had to lie next to the hearth in the ashes. This is why she always looked so dusty and dirty and why they called her Cinderella.

16

THE RIDDLE

"Bring this to your master," said the witch as she handed the servant a parting drink. But at that moment the glass broke, the poison splattered on the servant's horse, and it was so lethal the animal fell down dead on the spot. The servant ran after his master and told him what had happened, but the prince didn't want to abandon his saddle, so he sent the servant back to fetch it. When he came to the dead horse, a raven was already sitting there and eating it.

"Who knows if we'll be able to find anything better to eat today?" said the servant, and so he killed the raven and took it with him.

17

THE THREE SPINNERS

In her distress, the maiden went over to the window and saw three women coming in her direction: the first had a broad flat foot, the second had such a large lower lip that it hung down over her chin, and the third had an immense thumb. They stopped in front of her window and asked what the matter was. She told them about the impossible amount of flax she had to spin before she could marry the prince. If she failed, it would be the end of her.

"We'll spin it for you in no time at all," they said. "But only if you invite us to your wedding and are not ashamed of us. Moreover, you must call us your cousins and let us eat at your table."

"With all my heart," she responded. "Just come in and get to work right away!"

18

THE MOUSE, THE BIRD, AND THE SAUSAGE

For a long time they lived together in peace and happiness. The bird's job was to fly into the forest every day and bring back wood. The mouse had to carry water, light the fire, and set the table, while the sausage did the cooking.

Yet those who lead the good life are always looking for ways to make it even better. And, one day, as the bird was flying about, he met another bird and boasted about how wonderful his life was. But the other bird called him a poor sap because he had to do all the hard work, while his companions just enjoyed themselves at home with simple chores. The bird was disturbed by this, and the next day he refused to fly into the forest to do his work.

· 19 ·

THE BOOTS OF
BUFFALO LEATHER

"Pay attention, brother," said the soldier to the huntsman, "you're going to be amazed. I'm now going to make a toast to the health of these rogues." Next the soldier swung the bottle over the heads of the murderous robbers and cried out, "To your health, but open your mouths wide and raise your right hands in the air," and took a hearty swig. No sooner had he pronounced those words than the robbers all sat there motionless, as though they had been turned to stone. Their mouths were open and their right arms were raised in the air.

20

THE BREMEN TOWN
MUSICIANS

The animals discussed what they would have to do to drive the robbers out of the house. Finally they hit upon a plan. The donkey was to stand upright by the windowsill. The dog was to jump on the donkey's back, and the cat was to climb up the dog. When that was done, the rooster was to fly up and perch on the cat's head. After they put their plan into action, the signal was given, and they all started to make music together: The donkey brayed, the dog barked, the cat meowed, and the rooster crowed.

21

THE SINGING BONE

The older brother let the younger brother go ahead of him, and when the younger was halfway across, his brother gave him such a hard blow from behind that he fell down dead. After the older brother buried him under a bridge, he took the boar and brought it to the king, pretending he was the one who killed it. So the king gave him his daughter for his wife. When the younger brother never returned, the older said, "The boar probably ripped him apart." And everyone believed him.

22

THE DEVIL WITH THE
THREE GOLDEN HAIRS

On the other side of the river, the young man found the entrance to hell. It was dark and sooty inside, and the devil was not at home. However, the devil's grandmother was sitting in a large easy chair.

"What do you want?" she asked him, but she did not look very wicked.

"I'd like to have three golden hairs from the devil's head," he replied, "or else I won't be able to keep my wife."

"That's a lot to ask," she said. "If the devil comes home and finds you, it will cost you your neck. But, since I feel sorry for you, I'll see if I can help."

23

THE MAIDEN
WITHOUT HANDS

At midnight, as the king, the gardener, and the priest watched, the maiden came out of the bushes, walked over to the tree, and ate one of the pears with her mouth, while an angel in white stood next to her. The priest stepped forward and said to the maiden, "Have you come from heaven or from earth? Are you a spirit or a human being?"

"I'm not a spirit, but a poor creature forsaken by everyone except God."

"You may be forsaken by the whole world, but I shall not forsake you," said the king.

He took her with him to his royal palace, and since she was so beautiful and good, he loved her with all his heart, had silver hands made for her, and took her for his wife.

· 24 ·

FOUNDLING

"If you won't forsake me, I won't forsake you," said Lena.

"Never ever," said Foundling.

"Then change yourself into a church," said Lena, "and I'll be the chandelier hanging in it."

So when the three servants arrived to capture the two children, there was nothing to see but a church and a chandelier inside it.

"What's there to do here?" they sighed. "Let's go home."

25

THE WOLF AND THE
SEVEN YOUNG KIDS

The old mother goat sent the little kid home to fetch scissors, needle, and thread. Then she cut the wolf's belly open, and no sooner did she make the first cut than a kid stuck out his head. As she cut some more, all six of them jumped out, one after the other. They were all still alive and had not suffered the least bit of harm, for the monster's gluttony had been so great that he had swallowed them whole. What joy there was! They hugged their dear mother and hopped about like a tailor at his own wedding. But the old goat said, "Now go and look for some stones in the field. We'll fill the godless beast's belly with them while he's still asleep."

26

THE ELVES

The shoemaker and his wife hid themselves behind some clothes that were hanging in the corner of the room and watched closely. When it was midnight, two cute little naked elves scampered into the room, sat down at the shoemaker's workbench, took all the work that had been cut out, and began to stitch, sew, and hammer so skillfully and nimbly with their little fingers that the amazed shoemaker could not take his eyes off them. Indeed, they did not stop until everything was done and the shoes were left standing on the workbench. Then they quickly ran away.

27

LUCKY HANS

"I've got to walk all the way home carrying this large nugget," complained Hans. "Sure, it's gold, but it's so heavy that I can't keep my head straight, and my shoulder's been feeling the weight."

"I'll tell you what," said the passing horseman. "Let's exchange. I'll give you my horse, and you give me your gold nugget."

"Gladly," said Hans. "But let me warn you, it's a terribly heavy load to carry."

28

GAMBLING HANS

"Hans, come outside for a moment," said Death.

"Just wait a little while until I've finished at the gambling table," Hans responded. "In the meanwhile, why don't you climb that tree outside and pick a few things for us to nibble upon along the way?"

Death climbed the tree, but when he wanted to get down, he was unable to because it was enchanted, and Gambling Hans let him stay up there for seven years, during which time nobody died.

29

THE ROBBER BRIDEGROOM

"Could you tell me whether my bridegroom lives here?" asked the bride.

"Oh, you poor child," the old woman answered. "Do you realize where you are? This is a murderers' den! You think you're a bride soon to be celebrating your wedding, but the only marriage you'll celebrate will be with death. Just look! They ordered me to put this big kettle of water on the fire to boil. When they have you in their power, they'll chop you into pieces without mercy. Then they'll cook you and eat you."

The old woman then led the bride behind a large barrel, where nobody could see her. "Be as still as a mouse!" she warned.

30

GODFATHER DEATH

"I am Death, and I make all people equal."

"You're just the right one," said the man. "You take the rich and poor alike without making distinctions. I want you to be my child's godfather."

"I shall make your child rich and famous," Death answered. "Indeed, whoever has me for a friend shall never know any need."

THE JUNIPER TREE

My mother, she killed me.

My father, he ate me.

My sister, Marlene, she made sure to see

my bones were all gathered together,

bound nicely in silk, as neat as can be,

and laid beneath the juniper tree.

Tweet, tweet! What a lovely bird I am!

BRIER ROSE

The very moment she felt the prick of the spindle, the beautiful princess was overcome by a deep sleep. This sleep soon spread throughout the entire palace. The king and queen had just returned home, and when they entered the hall, they fell asleep, as did all the people of their court. Then the horses in the stable, the dogs in the courtyard, the pigeons on the roof, and the flies on the wall. Even the fire flickering in the hearth became quiet and fell asleep. The roast stopped sizzling, and the cook, who was just about to pull the kitchen boy's hair because he had done something wrong, let him go and fell asleep. Finally, the wind died down so that not a single leaf stirred on the trees outside the castle.

33

SNOW WHITE

The mirror spoke:

> *"You, my queen, may have a beauty quite rare,*
> *But Snow White is a thousand times more fair."*

The queen shuddered and became yellow and green with envy. From that hour on, her hate for the girl was so great that her heart throbbed and turned in her breast each time she saw Snow White. Like weeds, the envy and arrogance grew so dense in her heart that she no longer had any peace, day or night. Finally, she summoned a huntsman and said, "Take the child out into the forest, kill her, and bring me back her lungs and liver as proof of the deed."

34

THE SIX SWANS

Just when the sun was about to set, she heard rustling sounds and saw six swans come flying through the window. They landed on the floor and blew at each other until all their feathers were blown off. After that their swan skins slipped off like shirts. The maiden observed all this, and when she recognized her brothers, she rejoiced and crawled out from under the bed. Her brothers were delighted to see their little sister, but their joy was short-lived.

"We can only take off our swan skins for a quarter of an hour every evening," they told her. "After that we're changed back into swans."

Their sister wept and asked, "Can't you be set free?"

"We don't think so," they said. "You'd have to go six years without speaking or laughing, and during this time you'd have to sew six little shirts for us made of aster flowers. If just one word were to fall from your lips, then all the work would be for naught."

35

RUMPELSTILTSKIN

"If you don't spin this straw into gold by morning, then you must die," declared the king, and he locked her in the room all alone. The miller's poor daughter was close to her wits' end, for she knew nothing about spinning straw into gold, and her fear grew greater and greater. When she began to weep, the door suddenly opened, and a little man entered.

"Good evening, mistress miller, why are you weeping so?"

"Oh," answered the maiden, "I'm supposed to spin straw into gold, and I don't know how."

The little man then asked, "What will you give me if I spin it for you?"

36

MOTHER TRUDY

"What have you seen?" Mother Trudy asked the little girl.

"I saw a black man on your stairs."

"That was a charcoal burner."

"Then I saw a green man."

"That was a huntsman."

"After that I saw a bloodred man."

"That was a butcher."

"Oh, Mother Trudy, I was so petrified. I looked through the window and didn't see you, but I saw the devil with a fiery head."

"Oho!" said Mother Trudy. "Then you've seen the witch in her proper dress. I've been wanting you here and waiting for a long time. Now you shall provide me with light!"

Then she changed the girl into a block of wood and threw it into the fire.

· 37 ·

THE GOLDEN BIRD

"I'm going to tell you what to do," said the fox to the prince. "If you go straight ahead, you'll eventually come to a castle. In front of this castle there's a whole troop of soldiers sleeping on the ground, but don't pay any attention to them. Go right through the middle of their ranks and straight into the castle. Next, you're to go through all the rooms until you come to the chamber where the golden bird is hanging in a wooden cage. Nearby you'll also find a golden cage. But be careful not to take the bird out of its plain cage and put it into the splendid one. Otherwise you'll be in for trouble."

38

THE FOX AND THE CAT

"When the dogs are chasing after me, I can only save myself by scrambling up a tree," said the cat modestly.

"Is that all?" sneered the fox. "I've acquired over a hundred skills and have a bagful of tricks besides. You're so pitiful that you make me want to cry. But I'll take you with me and teach you how to get away from dogs."

Just at that moment a huntsman approached with four dogs. The cat sprang nimbly up a tree and sat on top, where the branches and leaves completely concealed her.

"Open your bag, Mr. Fox! Open your bag!" the cat called out to him, but the dogs had already pounced on him and held him tight.

39

LITTLE FARMER

Little Farmer promised the miller one final prediction and pressed the raven's head so that it cawed loudly.

"What did he say?" asked the miller.

"He said the devil's hiding in the hallway cupboard outside," replied Little Farmer.

"I want the devil out of there at once!" said the miller, and he unlocked the front door. The miller's wife was forced to hand over the keys before she could give warning to her hidden lover, and Little Farmer opened the cupboard. The priest ran out as fast as he could, and the miller exclaimed, "It's true! I saw the wicked scoundrel with my own eyes!"

40

ALL FUR

"Go see what kind of beast has hidden itself in that hollow tree," the king said to his huntsmen.

The hunstmen obeyed the king's command, and when they returned to him, they said, "There's a strange animal lying there asleep. We've never seen anything like it. Its skin is made up of a thousand different kinds of fur."

"See if you can catch it alive," said the king. "Then tie it to the wagon, and we'll take it with us."

When the huntsmen seized the creature, it woke up in a fright and cried to them, "I'm just a poor girl, forsaken by my mother and father! Please have pity on me and take me with you."

"You'll be perfect for the kitchen, *All Fur*," they said. "Come with us, and you can sweep up the ashes there."

41

SNOW WHITE AND ROSE RED

It did not take them long to all become accustomed to one another, and
the clumsy guest had to put up with the mischievous pranks of the girls.
They tugged his fur with their hands, planted their feet upon his back
and rolled him over, or they took a hazel switch and hit him. When
he growled, they just laughed. The bear took everything in good spirit.
Only when they became too rough did he cry out, "Let me live, children.

Snow White, Rose Red,

would you beat your suitor dead?"

42

JORINDA AND JORINGEL

Once upon a time there was an old castle in the middle of a great, dense forest, and an old woman lived there all by herself. During the day, she turned herself into a cat or a night owl, but in the evening she would return to her normal human form. She had the ability to lure game and birds, which she would slaughter and then roast. If any man came within a hundred steps of the castle, she would cast a spell over him so that he would not be able to move from the spot. If an innocent maiden came within her magic circle, the old woman would change her into a bird and stuff her in a wicker basket. She had well over seven thousand baskets with rare birds of this kind.

43

THE SINGING,
SPRINGING LARK

"I didn't know that the bird belonged to you," said the man. "I'll make up for my trespassing and give you a great deal of gold if only you'll spare my life."

"Nothing can save you," said the lion, "unless you promise to give me the first thing you meet when you get home. If you agree, then I'll not only grant your life, but I'll also give you the bird for your daughter."

At first the man refused, knowing how his youngest daughter always ran to him as soon as he returned home. But his servant was very scared of the lion and said, "It doesn't always have to be your daughter. Maybe it'll be a cat or a dog." And so the man let himself be persuaded and took the singing, springing lark.

44

HOW SIX MADE THEIR
WAY IN THE WORLD

"Just you wait!" said the soldier. "If I find the right people, I'll force the king to turn over all the treasures of his kingdom to me." And he set off down the road.

In the forest, he found a man tearing up six trees like blades of wheat. On a hill he found a huntsman who could shoot out the left eye of a fly two miles away. In a tree he found a man who could turn seven windmills by blowing through one nostril. In a field he met a one-legged man who could run faster than any bird could fly. In a valley he met a man with a magical cap who could turn everything around him to frost.

"Oh, come with me," said the soldier. "If we six stick together, we'll certainly make our way in the world!"

· 45 ·

THE GOOSE GIRL

The goose boy told the old king everything he had seen — that in the morning, when they drove the geese through the dark gateway, there was a horse's head nailed on the wall, and the goose girl always spoke to it: "Oh, poor Falada, I see you hanging there." And the head answered her:

> *"Dear Queen, is that you really there?*
> *Oh, if only your mother knew,*
> *her heart would break in two!"*

46

BEARSKIN

When the oldest daughter caught sight of him, she was so terribly frightened that she let out a shriek and ran away. The second examined him from head to foot and said, "How can I marry a man who no longer resembles a human being? I'd rather have a shaved bear trained to act like a man. At least it could wear a uniform and white gloves."

But the youngest daughter said, "He must be a good man to have helped our father out of trouble. If a bride has been promised to him in return, then I shall be the one."

It was a shame that Bearskin's face was covered with dirt and hair. Otherwise, one could have seen how his heart leapt for joy when he heard those words.

47

KING THRUSHBEARD

The disgraced princess ran out the door, ashamed by her poverty, but a man caught up with her on the stairs and brought her back. When she looked at him, she saw it was King Thrushbeard, and he said to her in a friendly way, "Don't be afraid. I and the poor minstrel who lived with you in the wretched cottage are one and the same person. I disguised myself out of love for you, and I was also the hussar who rode over your pots and smashed them to pieces. I did all that to humble your proud spirit and to punish you for the insolent way you behaved toward me."

48

THE TWO TRAVELERS

Mountains and valleys never meet, but people often do, especially the good and the bad. So it was that the paths of a shoemaker and a tailor crossed during their travels. The tailor was a handsome little fellow, always merry and in good spirits. When he saw the shoemaker coming from the other direction, he recognized him by his trade and decided to sing a little ditty to tease him. However, the shoemaker couldn't take a joke and made a sour face as if he had just drunk some vinegar. Indeed, he looked as if he would grab the little tailor by the scruff of the neck.

49

HANS MY HEDGEHOG

Once upon a time there was a farmer who had plenty of money, but rich as he was, his happiness was not complete: He had no children with his wife. When he went into town, other farmers often made fun of him and asked why he had no children. One day he finally got angry, and when he went home, he said, "I want to have a child, even if it's a hedgehog!"

Then his wife gave birth to a child whose upper half was hedgehog and bottom half was human. When she saw the child, she was horrified and said, "You see how you cursed us!"

"There's nothing we can do about it," said her husband. "The boy must be christened."

"There's only one name I can think of," said the wife, "and that's Hans My Hedgehog."

50

THE LITTLE SHROUD

"Oh, Mother, please stop weeping. Otherwise, I won't be able to get to sleep in my coffin. My little shroud is all wet from the tears you've been shedding on it."

THE STOLEN PENNIES

They ripped up the boards of the floor and found two pennies that the child had received from his mother when he was alive to give to a poor man. But the child had kept the pennies for himself and hidden them. However, he had not been able to rest in his grave and had come back every day at noon to look for the pennies. So the parents gave the money to a poor man, and after that the child was never seen again.

THE OLD MAN AND
HIS GRANDSON

When he sat at the table, he could barely hold his spoon, and often spilled soup on the tablecloth, while some of it would also drip from his mouth. His son and daughter-in-law found this disgusting and eventually forced the old grandfather to sit in a corner behind the stove and eat always from the same wooden bowl. Some time later, the small four-year-old grandson was piecing together some wooden planks on the ground.

"What are you doing?" asked the father.

"I'm making a little trough," answered the child. "You and mother shall eat out of it when I grow up."

· 53 ·

THE DEVIL'S
SOOTY BROTHER

"What's the matter?" asked the devil. "You look so gloomy."

"I'm hungry and have no money," said the soldier.

"If you hire yourself out to me as my servant," the devil said, "you'll have enough for the rest of your life. But you've got to serve me seven years, and after that you'll be free. There's just one thing I've got to tell you: You're not allowed to wash yourself, comb your hair, trim your beard, cut your nails or hair, or wipe your eyes."

"If that's the way it must be, let's get on with it," the soldier said, and followed the devil all the way to hell.

THE LETTUCE DONKEY

The lost huntsman picked out a fine head of lettuce and ate some of the leaves. No sooner had he taken a few bites than he had a strange sensation and felt completely changed: He sprouted four legs, a thick neck, and two long ears, and to his horror he saw that he had been transformed into a donkey. Nevertheless, since he still felt very hungry, he kept eating it with great zest. Eventually, he came to another kind of lettuce, and after he swallowed a few leaves, he felt a new kind of sensation and returned to his human form.

THE TURNIP

The farmer did not know what to do with the turnip, nor did he know whether it would bring him luck or misfortune. Finally he thought, If you sell it, you won't get anything worth much. And, if you eat it, you might as well eat the small turnips, which are just as good. The best thing would be to bring it to the king. That way you can honor him with a gift.

· 56 ·

ONE-EYE, TWO-EYES, AND THREE-EYES

There was a woman who had three daughters. The oldest was called One-Eye because she only had a single eye in the middle of her forehead. The second was called Two-Eyes because she had two eyes like all other human beings. The youngest was called Three-Eyes, and you can guess why.

Since Two-Eyes did not look any different from other people, her mother and sisters could not stand her. "You're no better than ordinary folk," they would say to her. "You don't belong to us!" They pushed her around and gave her shabby hand-me-down clothes to wear and only leftovers to eat. Whenever they could, they caused her as much grief as possible.

THE WORN-OUT DANCING SHOES

Once upon a time there was a king who had twelve daughters, each one more beautiful than the next. They slept together in a large room where their beds stood side by side, and in the evening, when they went to sleep, the king shut and locked the door. However, when he opened it in the morning, he would see that their shoes were worn from dancing, and nobody could discover how this kept happening. Finally, the king had it proclaimed that whoever could find out where his daughters danced during the night could choose one of them for his wife and eventually be king. But anyone who came and failed to uncover the secret after three days and nights would lose his life.

THE TWELVE HUNTSMEN

When the young women appeared before the princess, she ordered twelve hunting outfits made, each one just like the next, and the eleven young women had to put on the outfits, while she herself put on the twelfth. She then took leave of her father and rode away with the eleven young women until they came to the court of her former bridegroom, whom she loved so dearly. There she asked whether he needed any huntsmen and whether he would take all twelve of them into his service. The king looked at her and did not recognize her. But since they were fine-looking fellows, he said, yes, he would gladly employ them. And so they became the king's twelve huntsmen.

IRON HANS

As the dog approached the pool, a long, bare arm reached out of the water, grabbed the animal, and dragged it down. When the huntsman saw this, he went back to the castle and got three men to come with buckets and bail the water out of the pool. When they could see the bottom, they discovered a wild man lying there. His body was brown as rusty iron, and his hair hung over his face down to his knees. They bound the wild man with rope and led him away to the castle, where everyone was amazed by him. The king had him put in an iron cage and forbade anyone to open it under penalty of death. The queen herself was given the key for safekeeping.

MOTHER HOLLE

At last she came to a small cottage where an old woman was looking
out of a window. She had such big teeth that the maiden was scared and
wanted to run away. But the old woman cried after her, "Why are you
afraid, my dear child? Stay with me, and if you do all the housework
properly, everything will turn out well for you. Only you must make my
bed nicely and carefully and give it a good shaking so the feathers fly.
Then it will snow on earth, for I am Mother Holle."

THE GOOSE GIRL
AT THE SPRING

The young count began to have some doubts when the old woman mentioned an hour's walk, but she didn't let him renege on his offer to help. She lifted the sack onto his back and hung two baskets on his arms.

"You see," she said, "there's nothing to it."

"No, it's not light at all," responded the count with a pained expression on his face. "The bundle is very heavy. It feels as if it were packed with nothing but bricks, and the baskets feel as though they were made of lead. I can hardly breathe!" He would have liked to set everything down, but the old woman wouldn't let him.

"Just look," she cried mockingly, "the young gentleman won't carry what an old woman like me has so often hauled. Get a move on. Nobody's going to take that bundle off your back again."

· 62 ·

SIMELEI MOUNTAIN

He was about to leave the cave with his load of jewels, but his heart and mind had become so occupied by the treasures that he had forgotten the name of the mountain and called out, "Simelei Mountain, Simelei Mountain, open up!" But that was not the right name, and the mountain remained closed. Then he became frightened, and the more he tried to recall the name, the more confused his thoughts became, and the treasures were of no use to him at all.

LAZY HEINZ

Fat Trina was as lazy as her husband. "Dear Heinz," she said one day, "why should we make our lives so dreary and ruin the best years of our youth when there's no need for it? Wouldn't we be better off if we traded our two goats for a beehive? The goats disturb our sweetest sleep each morning with their bleating, plus bees don't have to be tended or taken out to pasture. They fly out and find their own way home again. Moreover, they gather honey by themselves, and we won't have to exert ourselves in the least."

· 64 ·

FITCHER'S BIRD

Finally, she came to the forbidden door. She wanted to walk past it, but curiosity got the better of her. She put the key into the lock, and the door sprang open. But what did she see when she entered? There was a large bloody basin in the middle of the room, and it was filled with dead people who had been chopped to pieces. Next to the basin was a block of wood with a glistening ax on top of it.

STRONG HANS

The abducted woman remained in the cave with the robbers for many years, forced to do all their housekeeping while raising her child as best she knew how. Hans grew big and strong. His mother told him stories and taught him how to read from an old book about knights, which she had found in the cave. When Hans was nine years old, he made a sturdy club out of a fir branch and hid it behind his bed. Then he went to his mother and said, "Dear Mother, tell me now, once and for all, who my father is. I've got to know."

· 66 ·

THE BLACKSMITH
AND THE DEVIL

The blacksmith said to the devil, "I want to make sure you're really the devil. Show me again how you can make yourself as large as a fir tree and as small as a mouse."

The devil was prepared and performed his feat. But just as he changed himself into a mouse, the blacksmith grabbed him and stuck him into his sack. Then the blacksmith cut off a stick from a nearby tree, threw the sack to the ground, and began beating the devil, who screamed pitifully and ran back and forth, unable to escape. Finally the blacksmith said, "I'll let you go if you give me the sheet from your large book on which I wrote my name."

THE BLUE LIGHT

The dwarf took the soldier by the hand and led him out of the well through an underground passage. Along the way the dwarf showed him the treasures that the witch had gathered and hidden there, and the soldier took as much gold as he could carry. When he was back above ground, he said to the dwarf, "Now go and tie up the old witch and bring her to court."

It was not long before she came riding by, quick as the wind. She was tied to the back of a wildcat and screaming in a frightful manner. Soon after that the dwarf returned alone.

"It's all as you wished," he said. "The witch is already hanging on the gallows. What more do you command, master?"

THE NIXIE IN THE POND

The hunstman did not realize that he was close to the dangerous millpond, and after he had skinned and gutted the deer, he went to the water to wash his hands, which were covered with blood. No sooner did he dip his hands into the water than the nixie rose up and embraced him laughingly with her sopping wet arms. Then she dragged him down into the water so quickly that only the clapping of the waves above could be heard.

THE DOG AND
THE SPARROW

At last the wagoner, furious and blind with rage, caught the sparrow with his hand.

"Do you want me to kill it?" his wife asked.

"No!" he yelled. "That would be too merciful. This pest has spilled my wine, blinded my horses, eaten my wheat, and destroyed my home. I want it to die a cruel death. I'm going to swallow it."

Then he took the bird and swallowed him whole. However, the sparrow began to flutter inside his body and fluttered back up again into the man's mouth. Once there he stuck out his head and repeated his cry, "Wagoner, you ran over my good friend the dog and killed him! Now it will cost you your life!"

THE WEDDING OF MRS. FOX

Once upon a time there was an old fox with nine tails who believed his wife was unfaithful to him and wanted to put her to the test. So he stretched himself out under the bench, kept perfectly still, and pretended to be dead as a doornail.

THE MASTER THIEF

"Ah, Father," replied the son, "the young tree was not bound to a post and grew up crooked. Now it's too old and will never become straight again. How is it that I appear before you as such a wealthy gentleman? I became a thief. But don't be alarmed. I am a master thief. There's no such thing as locks or bolts for me. Whatever my heart desires is mine. But I don't want you to think that I am a common criminal. I only take from the rich, who have more than they need, and prefer only to give to the poor. Therefore, I won't touch a thing that doesn't demand effort, cunning, and skill to obtain it."

THE THIEF AND HIS MASTER

When the maid took the bridle off, the apprentice changed from a horse to a sparrow and flew out the door. Seeing this, the master also became a sparrow and flew after him. They met and held a contest in midair, but the master lost and fell into the water, where he turned himself into a fish. The boy also turned himself into a fish, and they held another contest. Once again the master lost, and turned himself into a rooster, while the boy changed himself into a fox and bit the master's head off. And so the master has remained dead up to this very day.

THE WATER OF LIFE

"Oh, we know you found the Water of Life," said the two wicked older brothers, "but we're the ones who've received the reward for all your trouble. You should have been smarter and kept your eyes open. We took the water from you when you fell asleep at sea, and in a year's time one of us will fetch the beautiful princess. Still, you had better not expose us. Father will not believe you anyway, and if you breathe a single word about it, your life will be worth nothing. If you keep quiet, we'll let you live."

· 74 ·

THE MOON

When the moon was reassembled in the underworld, where darkness had always reigned, the dead became restless and awoke from their sleep. They were astounded to find that they could see again: The moonlight was as bright as the sun to their weak eyes. They got up, became merry, and assumed their old ways of life again. Some began to play and dance. Others went to the taverns, where they asked for wine, got drunk, brawled, and quarreled. The noise became greater and greater until it finally reached as far as heaven.

THUMBLING

"How sad that we have no children!" said the poor farmer. "It's so quiet here, and other homes are full of noise and life."

"Yes," his wife responded with a sigh. "If only we had a child, just one, even if it were tiny and no bigger than my thumb, I'd be quite satisfied. We'd surely love him with all our hearts."

Now it happened that the wife fell sick, and after seven months she gave birth to a child that was indeed perfect in every way but no bigger than a thumb.

"It's just as we wished," they said, "and he shall be dear to our hearts."

AFTERWORD

Shaun Tan

Like many children I knew the stories of the Brothers Grimm primarily as visual images: Disney movies, of course, as well as a number of elaborately illustrated books from my family's local library. Scenes of green forests, snow, mountains, and castles were all wonderfully exotic, but could not have been further from my childhood reality, growing up along the semi-arid coastal plain of Western Australia. The Brothers Grimm stood for escapist fantasy, more delight than darkness, especially in these more sanitized and decorative versions.

It's only as an adult that I've really come to appreciate these tales for their complexity, ambiguity, and endurance. As a writer and artist, I often wonder if my own stories will have much staying power and frequently look to older examples for inspiration and instruction — "breaking bread with the dead" as Auden put it. In the case of successful fairy tales — those that we continue to remember and retell — there's such a strange mix of irrationality and logic, all wrapped up in a dream-like brevity (as if a more elaborate version might break the spell of sleeping reason) and there's a strong sense in every story collected by the Brothers Grimm that the separation between waking and dreaming worlds is actually quite thin, that they bleed into each other naturally enough. It may be that all timeless tales and mythologies resonate through this kind of tension. Strung between the real and unreal, the literal and impossible, convincing and absurd, these tales of nameless princes, peasants, stepsisters, and witches remain constantly intriguing, not least because they are often a little disturbing and hard to explain.

The same is true of the best folk art, and in creating my own illustrations for *The Singing Bones* I was much inspired by Inuit stone carvings and pre-Columbian clay figurines (following trips to Canada and Mexico respectively). These exhibit a wonderful blend of whimsy and seriousness, and a well-considered marriage of earthy material — stone and clay that never pretend to be anything but stone and clay — infused with weightless and magical ideas. The result is a kind of fossilized narrative, worn by multiple "tellings" into a comfortable shape that often fits nicely in the hand — the edges rubbed off, as Neil Gaiman puts it, and somehow reassuring — something I tried to achieve with my own sculptures, which are generally about the size and weight of an orange.

The main materials I've used are papier-mâché and air-drying clay, carved back and painted with acrylics, oxidized metal powder, wax, and shoe polish. The resistance of clay in particular at a small scale encourages simplicity, especially where the key tools are blunt fingers and thumbs: Faces and gestures are abbreviated, just like characters in the tales themselves. The concept of a thing also becomes more important than a detailed likeness: A fox need only be a few red triangles, a sleeping man requires no body, and a queen's face can be eroded away by the force of a single, elemental feeling: jealousy. What matters above all else are the hard bones of the story, and I wanted many of these objects to appear as if they've emerged from an imaginary archaeological dig, and then been sparingly illuminated as so many museum objects are, as if a flashlight beam has passed momentarily over some odd objects resting in the dark galleries of our collective subconscious. Like the tales themselves, they might brighten in our imagination without surrendering any of their original enigma.

ANNOTATED INDEX

The following index includes brief summaries of Grimms' fairy tales for those curious to know a little more about each story. These are, of course, no substitute for the full tales themselves in various retold forms, the sources of which can be found in the further reading list that follows, while complete texts of most tales can also be found online.

1 THE FROG KING

When a princess loses her favorite golden ball in a deep well, a frog fetches it in return for her promise of love and companionship. Afterward, she wants to break her promise, but her stern father compels her to keep her word. However, the princess is so disgusted by the frog that she eventually throws it against a wall. In doing so, she breaks a spell and the frog turns into a handsome young prince.

2 THE COMPANIONSHIP OF THE CAT AND THE MOUSE

A cat and a mouse decide to share a house together and buy a pot of fat to see them through the winter. After hiding the pot in a nearby church, the cat tells the mouse that he must attend a number of kitten christenings, but each time he secretly eats a little of the fat. When the mouse finally discovers the empty pot and accuses the cat of betraying their friendship, the cat devours her because that's the way of the world.

3 HANSEL AND GRETEL

Abandoned in the forest by their impoverished parents due to a great famine in the country, Hansel and Gretel become lost and discover a house made of bread, cake, and sugar, unaware that it belongs to an evil witch who cooks and eats children. Although captured, they use their wits to trick the witch, burning her to death in her own oven and then escaping to be reunited with their father.

4 LITTLE RED CAP

On her way to deliver wine and cake to her ailing grandmother, a naive young maiden meets a cunning wolf and tells him all about her errand. Upon reaching her destination, she questions her grandmother's unusual appearance, at which point the disguised wolf leaps out of bed and eats her. A passing huntsman discovers what has happened and cuts open the wolf's stomach to free the maiden and her grandmother, both alive and wiser from their ordeal.

5 THE BOY WHO LEFT HOME TO FIND OUT ABOUT FEAR

A naive young boy who couldn't learn anything sets out in the world to learn how to get the creeps because he doesn't understand them. Despite experiencing many horrifying encounters, he survives and manages to win the hand of a princess because of his naive fearlessness. Only when his new wife throws a bucket of fish over him in bed does he finally learn what it means to have the creeps.

6 FAITHFUL JOHANNES

The royal servant Johannes promises to fulfill his king's dying wish to never allow his son's gaze to fall upon the portrait of a beautiful foreign princess. But when the young king happens to view the painting, he falls obsessively in love with her. Ever faithful, Johannes then devotes himself to helping his new master win the heart of the princess while protecting him from disaster. However, the young king causes Johannes to turn into stone when he doubts the loyalty of the servant. Only by sacrificing his own children does the king manage to revive Johannes, who then revives the children as reward.

7   THE TWELVE BROTHERS

A king who has twelve sons decides he will execute them if his thirteenth child is a girl, so that she might inherit the kingdom. Fearful of the consequences, the queen urges her sons to disappear forever into the forest when their sister is born. Many years later, the young girl discovers the dark family secret and sets out to look for her brothers. Once she discovers them, she inadvertently causes them to be turned into ravens and must keep silent for seven years to allow them to return to their human forms. In turn, her brothers save her from an unjust punishment.

8   THE WHITE SNAKE

A curious servant steals a taste of a king's secret dish — a mysterious white snake — and is suddenly able to understand the language of animals. He sets off traveling and rescues several distressed animals along the way. Later, they return each of his favors by helping their human friend accomplish three difficult tasks required to win the love of a princess: The fish retrieve a lost ring, the ants collect millet, and the ravens retrieve a golden apple from the Tree of Life.

9   LITTLE BROTHER AND LITTLE SISTER

Two orphans are continually abused by their stepmother, who is a witch. They decide to run away into a forest, where the little brother is turned into a deer when he drinks water from a bewitched stream. However, his sister will not abandon him, even after she marries a king. Their strong bond of love protects them from the witch who pursues them jealously. Even murder cannot dissolve their union, and justice eventually prevails: The witch is burned at the stake, and the little brother regains his human form.

10   RAPUNZEL

A sorceress takes the child of a hapless couple because they steal rapunzel lettuce from her garden. She raises the baby, who becomes a beautiful young woman named Rapunzel, and keeps her imprisoned in a doorless tower for her own protection. Only the sorceress can reach her by calling out for her to let down her long, golden locks, which the sorceress then uses to climb up to the solitary window. A prince happens to pass by and discovers this secret. So, he scales the tower and instantly falls in love. When the witch discovers Rapunzel is pregnant, both lovers are mercilessly punished and separated. They are ultimately reunited after years of loneliness and misery.

11   THE THREE LITTLE GNOMES IN THE FOREST

A kind and generous maiden meets three little gnomes in a forest. After she helps them, they cast a spell on her, causing gold coins to fall from her mouth when she speaks. When her wicked and greedy stepsister meets the gnomes, she refuses to help them, and toads jump out of her mouth instead. The virtuous girl marries a king, only to be murdered by her jealous sister and stepmother. When the king magically resurrects his queen and the truth is revealed, the offenders are executed.

12   THE THREE SNAKE LEAVES

A soldier agrees to marry an old king's beautiful daughter, who demands that if one of them were to die first, the other must be buried alongside. So, when the young queen falls ill and dies, her husband is obliged to join her in the crypt. There the young king witnesses one snake resurrect another by using three magical leaves, and he revives his wife the same way. Ungrateful, she later has an affair with a ship's captain, and together they murder the husband while at sea. Using the snake leaves, however, the young king's servant resurrects his master, and together they reveal the truth to the old king, who sentences the treacherous young queen and her accomplice to drown at sea.

13   THE FISHERMAN AND HIS WIFE

When a poor fisherman catches a fish that claims to be an enchanted prince, he decides to let it go. His unhappy wife demands that he return and ask the magic fish for a nice cottage because they live in a hovel. After her request is granted by the fish, she remains unsatisfied and demands that her husband ask the fish for a castle. Afterward, she wants to become king, emperor, and then pope. Each wish is dutifully granted, but the fisherman's wife remains unsatisfied. Finally, she asks to be like God, at which point the fish takes everything away, returning the fisherman and his wife to their original poverty.

14   THE BRAVE LITTLE TAILOR

After swatting seven flies all at once, a little tailor is overcome with pride and travels the world announcing his achievement: "seven with one blow!" He meets a giant who tests the tailor's claims of strength, but is outwitted by the clever little man again and again. As his fame spreads, the tailor confidently tricks other giants into slaying one another, captures a wild beast at a king's request, wins the hand of a princess, and terrifies would-be assassins, all by using his wits alone.

15   CINDERELLA

Persecuted by an evil stepmother and two stepsisters, a young maiden is forced into lowly subservience, made to lie in hearth ashes and derisively named "Cinderella." Prevented from attending a royal festival by her stepmother, Cinderella disguises herself in a beautiful dress and slippers, courtesy of a magical bird that appears above her mother's grave. She manages to find her way to the festival, where the prince is to choose a bride after three nights. When the prince encounters Cinderella, he is smitten by her, but Cinderella's true identity remains a mystery until a lost golden slipper is found that, despite the false claims of her stepsisters, fits her foot alone. In the end she marries the prince, and her stepsisters have their eyes pecked out by vengeful birds.

16   THE RIDDLE

A traveling prince and his faithful servant encounter a witch living in a forest. The witch tries to poison the prince, but his horse is killed instead. The servant catches a raven as it eats the horse's carcass, and later asks an innkeeper to cook the bird for himself and the prince. Instead, the wicked innkeeper shares the cooked bird with his friends, who are murderous thieves, and they are all killed by the tainted meat. The surviving prince later wins the hand of a princess by challenging her to a difficult riddle concerning the poisoned raven: "One slew nobody and yet slew twelve."

17   THE THREE SPINNERS

A mother lies to a passing queen, saying that her lazy daughter is a prolific worker at a spinning wheel. Impressed, the queen demands that the girl spin a roomful of flax in return for marriage to her son, a task only made possible by the unexpected arrival of three deformed women with exceptional skills. They tell the lazy girl that they will help her if she invites them to her wedding as her cousins and does not act ashamed of them. As guests at the wedding, the three spinners tell the king their deformities were caused by years of spinning, and, consequently, he forbids the new princess from ever again doing such work.

18   THE MOUSE, THE BIRD, AND THE SAUSAGE

A mouse, a bird, and a sausage live together in harmony, each responsible for set tasks. The bird collects wood, the mouse lights a fire to boil water, and the sausage cooks and seasons their daily soup. One day the bird, disturbed by criticism of their lifestyle by another bird, suggests that they all exchange roles. The results are disastrous: The sausage is eaten by a dog while out collecting wood; the mouse drowns as he tries to cook the soup; and the bird starts an uncontrollable fire and dies trying to put it out.

19   THE BOOTS OF BUFFALO LEATHER

A courageous soldier, who has been discharged from the army and is down on his luck, meets a lost huntsman in a forest, and the two travel together. Desperately hungry, they seek hospitality at a nearby house only to find a den of murderous thieves. The soldier boldly sits down at their dinner table, much to the huntsman's horror, suggesting they be allowed to eat before being killed, to which the startled thieves agree. But during a toast, the soldier hypnotizes the thieves and then calls his past comrades to cart them to prison. Upon reaching the city, the huntsman reveals himself to be none other than the king and rewards the soldier for his deeds.

20   THE BREMEN TOWN MUSICIANS

Four elderly animals — a donkey, a dog, a cat, and a rooster — escape abusive domestic lives and together seek their fortune as town musicians. On the road to the town of Bremen, they come upon a house occupied by robbers and, standing one atop the other, they bray, bark, meow, and crow through a window. Overcome by fear and superstition, the men flee their hideout, and the animals take over the house and live there comfortably forever after.

21   THE SINGING BONE

Two brothers accept a king's challenge to rid his forest of a dangerous boar. The diligent younger brother succeeds in killing the animal, but is in turn slain by his jealous older brother, who conceals the crime and marries the princess as reward. Many years later, a bone of the dead brother is found by a shepherd and fashioned into a horn that sings of the betrayal. When the king hears this song, he orders the remaining bones to be recovered for churchyard burial, and the murderous brother is sewn up in a sack and drowned.

22   THE DEVIL WITH THE THREE GOLDEN HAIRS

An evil king tries to kill a poor young man prophesied to take over his kingdom. After this young man, known as fortune's favorite, manages to marry the king's daughter, the king demands that he fetch three golden hairs from the head of the devil. When the young man arrives in hell, the devil is not at home. Instead, fortune's favorite meets the devil's grandmother, who takes pity on him and offers to help him. While the devil dozes on her lap, she plucks the hairs herself and distracts him with conversation. The young man returns victorious and, having overheard a few secrets from the devil, he tricks the king into giving up his kingdom.

23   THE MAIDEN WITHOUT HANDS

A miller unwittingly promises his daughter to the devil, but when the girl proves too pious to snare, the devil bullies the miller into cutting off her hands with an ax. The maiden leaves home and wanders throughout the land accompanied by a guardian angel. One night a king discovers her eating pears in his garden, and the two fall in love and marry. Shortly after, the king must go off to war and, during his absence, the young queen gives birth to a baby son. Meanwhile, the devil returns and tricks the king's mother into believing that her son wants his wife and baby to be killed. The old mother refuses to do this and sends the maiden away to live with her child in the wilderness. Later the king discovers the devil's treachery and, after years of searching, he finds his wife and son living in a forest with an angel. Trust is restored, and they joyfully return home.

24   FOUNDLING

A forester finds a small child in a tree and raises him as "Foundling," much loved by his own child Lena. One day Lena learns that their old cook plans to boil Foundling in a pot, so the two secretly run away. The cook sends servants after them, but the children hide by magically changing themselves first into a rosebush in bloom and then into a church with a chandelier. When the cook comes after them herself, Foundling turns into a pond and Lena turns into a duck. As the cook stops to drink the water, the duck grabs her by the head and pulls her to a watery death.

25   THE WOLF AND THE SEVEN YOUNG KIDS

Left at home by their mother goat, seven young kids are told to beware of a wolf who might try to trick his way into the house. They successfully repel his attempts until the wolf perfects a disguise, gets inside, and eats all but the youngest kid, who hides in a clock and later tells his distraught mother what has happened. She tracks down the sleeping wolf, cuts his stomach open to free her children, and fills the cavity with rocks. The wolf falls into a well trying to quench his thirst, and the goats dance with joy.

26   THE ELVES

A struggling shoemaker is astounded to find perfectly made shoes assembled from pieces left on his workbench overnight. This happens again and again, and the shoes sell for a handsome profit. Intrigued, he and his wife keep vigil one night and observe two cute, naked elves doing all the work. The shoemaker and his wife leave a gift of tiny clothes and shoes as thanks, which the elves receive with great delight. Then they dance out the door, never to be seen again.

27   LUCKY HANS

After serving his master for seven years, Hans is paid a gold nugget as big as his head. It proves very heavy to carry, and Hans willingly exchanges it for a horse he can ride. He later exchanges the horse for a cow, whose milk he can drink. Then the cow for a pig, the pig for a goose, and the goose for a millstone, tricked each time by unscrupulous opportunists. But Hans is delighted by each transaction, and even when he loses the millstone, he considers it great luck to have been freed of the burden and runs all the way home.

28   GAMBLING HANS

Having gambled away all his possessions, Hans is visited by the Lord and Saint Peter, and his hospitality earns him three wishes. So he requests a deck of cards that enable him to always win, dice that enable him to always win, and a tree with many fruits that nobody can climb out of without his permission. Hans becomes invincible at the gambling table and is on the verge of winning half the world when the Lord and Saint Peter feel compelled to send Death to stop him. However, Hans tricks Death into climbing the magical tree, where he must remain for a long time. Later, Hans out-gambles Lucifer in hell and then sets his sights on conquering heaven. Not knowing what else to do, the Lord and Saint Peter smash Hans's soul into fragments, and these continue to infect the hearts of gamblers all over the world.

29   THE ROBBER BRIDEGROOM

A young maiden, fearful of the handsome bridegroom her father has chosen for her, reluctantly visits his home deep in a forest. There she meets an old woman who warns her that her bridegroom is one of several robbers, all murderous cannibals, and hides the girl behind a barrel. While witnessing the murder of another victim, a severed finger falls into the maiden's lap. The robbers soon fall asleep, and she is able to escape unnoticed. Later at their wedding, the maiden tells all to the assembled guests, showing the finger as proof. The band of murderers are promptly brought to justice and executed.

30   GODFATHER DEATH

A man looking for a godfather for his newborn son decides that Death is the best choice as he "makes all people equal" and promises wealth and fame. The boy grows up to become a famous doctor when Death shows him how to use an herb that can cure all ills, but he can only use it as Death commands. When the young doctor is summoned to treat a beautiful princess, he falls in love and refuses his godfather's request to let her die. Angered by this disobedience, Death takes the life of his godson instead.

31   THE JUNIPER TREE

A wicked stepmother beheads her young stepson out of spite and jealousy. Then she tricks her own daughter into accepting responsibility. The mother then cooks the body into a stew for her unwitting husband to consume. The boy's bones are gathered by his grieving stepsister, who buries them under a sacred juniper tree, and a bird magically appears on its branches. Then the bird flies off and travels the land, singing aloud of the murder. Along its way the bird gathers a gold chain, shoes, and a millstone from the townsfolk. The chain and shoes are gifts for the father and sister, and the bird drops the millstone on the evil stepmother's head. As she perishes, the boy appears alive and well.

32 BRIER ROSE

When twelve wise women are invited by a king to celebrate the birth of a princess, a thirteenth wise woman feels insulted by the lack of invitation and consequently curses the child to die upon pricking her finger with a spindle at the age of fifteen. However, one of the other wise women modifies the curse so that the young princess will sleep for one hundred years instead of dying — and so it comes to pass. Not only the princess, but the entire castle, is suspended in time, and a thick brier hedge grows around it so that nobody can reach the castle, though many princes die trying. After one hundred years, a fearless young prince arrives to find the hedge in bloom, and it opens before him. Then he searches the enchanted castle until he finds the princess and breaks the spell with his kiss. The two fall in love with each other, marry, and live happily ever after.

33 SNOW WHITE

When a queen learns from a talking mirror that she is not the "fairest of all" in the realm, she is driven mad with jealousy and orders a huntsman to murder her stepdaughter, Snow White, whose beauty is "a thousand times more fair." But the huntsman allows the maiden to escape into the forest, where she is taken in by seven kind dwarves. The queen transforms herself into an old crone, visits Snow White while the dwarves are out, and poisons her with an apple. The dwarves place Snow White's body in a glass coffin, and soon after a prince happens to pass by their cottage and falls in love with Snow White. The dwarves allow him to take the coffin with him, and Snow White is accidentally brought back to life when the piece of poisoned apple is jarred from her mouth. At the subsequent wedding, the evil queen is made to wear red-hot iron slippers and dance until she dies.

34 THE SIX SWANS

Six brothers from a king's first marriage are transformed into swans by the spiteful new queen. Their sister goes in search of them, and to break the evil spell she must sew six shirts from flowers and endure a six-year vow of silence. A king finds her and marries her because of her beauty. But she is repeatedly persecuted by the queen mother, accused of murdering her children, and sentenced to death. Just before she is executed, the sister finishes the shirts and completes her vow of silence. The brothers return to human form and their sister is free to speak out. As a result, the queen mother is then burned at the stake in her place.

35 RUMPELSTILTSKIN

Upon hearing a miller lie about his daughter's amazing ability to spin straw into gold, a king imprisons the maiden in his castle and demands she do just that, or else face execution. An imp-like creature appears and offers to do the work in exchange for a series of gifts, including the maiden's firstborn child. The miller's daughter agrees and becomes queen. When she eventually gives birth, the imp returns. But he takes pity on the queen, and will let her keep the child if she can guess his name in three days' time. On the third day the queen fortunately learns the imp's name from a court messenger, and correctly answers "Rumpelstiltskin," whereupon the enraged creature stamps and tears his own body in half.

36 MOTHER TRUDY

A disobedient little girl ignores her parents' warning about evil Mother Trudy and decides to visit her house anyway. Once there she sees a black man, a green man, and a bloodred man on the stairs of Mother Trudy's house and becomes frightened. But Mother Trudy explains they are nothing but a charcoal burner, a huntsman, and a butcher. When the girl describes having seen the devil with a fiery head, Mother Trudy reveals her true nature and takes great delight in turning the girl into firewood and warming herself as it burns brightly.

37 THE GOLDEN BIRD

When a golden bird is discovered to have stolen golden apples from a palace tree, a king charges his three sons with the task of hunting it down. Each son encounters a fox offering cryptic advice, but only the youngest prince takes heed. So begins a complicated adventure during which the prince makes several mistakes and is cheated by his two brothers. Each time the fox faithfully rescues him, until the bird is finally captured and the prince marries a beautiful princess. In return for his help, the fox requests that the prince shoot him dead and cut off his head and paws, an act that breaks a spell and restores his original human form, revealing that he is the princess's long-lost brother.

38 THE FOX AND THE CAT

An arrogant fox is dismissive of a cat who only knows how to climb up a tree, while boasting that he himself can evade dogs in a hundred clever ways. But when a hunting pack suddenly appears, the fox is caught while the cat escapes by climbing up a tree. Once safe in the branches, the cat chides the doomed fox.

39 LITTLE FARMER

Using his wits, Little Farmer trades a wooden calf for a real cow, whose hide he takes to sell in town. Along the way he finds an injured raven and takes shelter from a storm in a miller's home. There he observes that the miller's wife is having an illicit affair with a priest. When the miller returns home unexpectedly, Little Farmer claims to own a clairvoyant raven and earns himself a small fortune by exposing the priest as a "devil" hiding in a cupboard. Back home Little Farmer lies about his wealth and is accused of fraud by all the other villagers jealous of his good fortune. He tricks his way out of execution and then fools the entire village of accusers into drowning themselves.

40 ALL FUR

A princess is mortified by the incestuous desire of her father and flees into a forest dressed in a cloak made of a thousand kinds of pelts and furs, her hands and face blackened with soot beyond recognition. Another king discovers her while hunting and takes her to his castle where she becomes a lowly kitchen hand called "All Fur." When a royal ball is held, the princess secretly attends, clean and finely attired. Her beauty dazzles the king, and although she departs before her true identity can be discovered, she leaves small treasures in the king's soup as clues to her true identity. When the truth is revealed, the king marries the princess, and they live happily together until death.

41 SNOW WHITE AND ROSE RED

The inseparable sisters, Snow White and Rose Red, live together peacefully with their mother in a forest cottage. One cold night a bear seeks shelter with them, and they soon become close friends. After the bear leaves to guard a forest treasure, the sisters encounter a nasty old dwarf whom they rescue three times, only to receive his rage and ingratitude. When the bear suddenly appears, the cowardly dwarf offers up the little girls as a meal to protect himself, whereupon the bear strikes him dead. As soon as he does this, the bear reveals himself to be a handsome prince and explains that the wicked dwarf had cast him under a spell and stolen his treasures. Now that the dwarf is dead, he marries Snow White, while his brother weds Rose Red. Together they share the dwarf's pillaged treasure and live happily ever after.

42 JORINDA AND JORINGEL

A sorceress living in a forest castle can transform herself into a cat or owl to hunt game, including young maidens, whom she captures, changes into songbirds, and keeps in a vast collection of cages. When the beautiful Jorinda is one such victim, her lover, Joringel, searches the land for a flower that appears to him in a dream. Upon finding it, he returns to the castle, defeats the sorceress, and rescues Jorinda along with thousands of other captured maidens.

43 THE SINGING, SPRINGING LARK

After unwittingly trying to steal a singing, springing lark from a ferocious lion's tree, a man is compelled to promise his daughter to the terrifying beast. However, the lion turns out to be a kind prince, able to sustain human form only at night, and so the young woman and beast are happily married. But when his wife accidentally exposes her lion-husband to candlelight, the prince is cursed to wander the world as a dove for seven years, pursued by his devoted wife. Along the way she is helped by the sun, moon, and winds, and their advice enables her to rescue her beloved from the spell of a foreign princess. In the end the two return home and live happily ever after.

44 HOW SIX MADE THEIR WAY IN THE WORLD

A soldier is unfairly discharged by a king and then seeks justice by gathering together a team of extraordinary individuals, each with superhuman powers: speed, sharp-shooting, strength, and the power to create strong winds and frost. Working together, they defeat the king's daughter in a footrace, overcome several challenges set by the deceitful king, cleverly escape his attempts to have them killed, and finally force him into surrendering all the wealth of his kingdom.

45 THE GOOSE GIRL

A beautiful princess is forced by her wicked chambermaid to exchange clothes and horses on their way to meet a foreign prince, and she must also vow never to reveal the deception. The prince ends up marrying the chambermaid while the true princess works as a lowly goose girl. To ensure silence, the chambermaid has the royal knacker kill the princess's faithful horse, Falada, whose head is then nailed to a wall. But the head continues to speak the truth whenever the goose girl passes by, and this strange incident is witnessed by the young boy Conrad, who tends the geese with her. Conrad tells the old king, who then learns the entire truth about the princess's identity. Once the old king knows everything, he has the chambermaid violently executed, and the prince marries his true bride.

46   BEARSKIN

A discharged soldier is abandoned by his hard-hearted brothers when he returns home after a war has ended. Impoverished, the soldier makes a deal with the devil. For seven years he must wear only the skin of a bear and never wash or groom himself. Soon he looks like a terrifying monster. However, thanks to the devil, the soldier's pockets are always full of gold that he uses to help the poor. At one point during his travels, "Bearskin" gives money to an old man so he can pay his debts, and in return, the man offers to let him wed one of his three daughters. Two of the daughters are disgusted by Bearskin and treat him with contempt, but the third agrees to marry him. When the seven years expire, the devil comes and washes the soldier clean so that he can present himself as a handsome man to his bride. The bride's sisters are driven mad with jealousy, and the devil takes their souls.

47   KING THRUSHBEARD

A proud and beautiful princess ridicules multiple suitors, including a good king whom she mocks for having a chin like a thrush's beak. From then on everyone calls him King Thrushbeard. Her father, frustrated by her arrogance, vows that she will marry the first beggar who comes to the palace door. So when a poor minstrel appears, the princess is forced to marry him, live in a forest hovel, and work for a living by making pots. When these are broken by a drunken hussar at the marketplace, she must work as a lowly kitchen maid in a king's castle. Soon after the king pretends to hold a wedding, she is humiliated and tries to run home. But the king is actually King Thrushbeard and reveals himself to have been the minstrel and the hussar all along and wants her to be his queen. Now humbled and contrite, the princess marries the king.

48   THE TWO TRAVELERS

A cheerful tailor meets a dour shoemaker, and they travel the road together. After a wrong turn in a forest, the tailor runs out of bread. The sadistic shoemaker offers help, but only if his companion will agree to have his eyes cut out. So the tailor is fed, blinded, and abandoned. However, he learns to see again when two poor sinners hanging from the gallows reveal how he might restore his sight from fresh dew. Then he goes on to work in a royal court where the shoemaker is also employed. Since the shoemaker has a guilty conscience, he tries to have the tailor expelled, but the tailor outsmarts him with the help of many animals he had befriended on the road. The shoemaker ends up having his eyes pecked out by crows.

49   HANS MY HEDGEHOG

A rich farmer and his wife are childless, and one day the frustrated farmer wishes for a child even if the baby were to be a hedgehog. Shortly thereafter his wife gives birth to a half-hedgehog boy. His parents raise him with shame and resentment. So, Hans My Hedgehog goes to live alone in a forest, happily tending livestock, playing bagpipes, and riding a rooster. A king gets lost in the forest and promises to give Hans the first thing that meets him when he returns home, and it turns out to be his daughter. A second lost king promises Hans the same thing. The first king breaks his promise, and Hans punishes his daughter by striking her with his quills. The second king honors the agreement, and his kindhearted daughter marries Hans, who then sheds his hedgehog skin at night and is transformed into a handsome young man. The skin is burned so that he never has to wear it again.

50   THE LITTLE SHROUD
When the ghost of a child appears to implore his inconsolable mother to stop crying over his death, she abides and bears her grief with patient silence. The child appears once more to thank her before lying to rest in his grave.

51   THE STOLEN PENNIES
A family friend who has been invited to a noon meal witnesses a small child repeatedly enter another room in the home and rummage in the cracks of the floorboards. When he describes this to his hosts, the wife recognizes the boy as the ghost of her recently deceased son, who had stolen two pennies and hidden them under the boards while alive. He had been asked to give the pennies to a poor man but instead had kept them for himself. The pennies are recovered and given to another poor man, and the ghost never returns.

52   THE OLD MAN AND HIS GRANDSON
A feeble old man embarrasses his son and daughter-in-law because he can barely hold his spoon at the dinner table. He is forced to eat alone in a corner from a wooden bowl. When his little grandson begins to build a wooden trough for his parents to eat from when they are elderly, his mother and father are shamed. The old man is immediately brought back to the family table.

53   THE DEVIL'S SOOTY BROTHER
An unemployed soldier hires himself out to the devil for seven years, during which time he must never wash or groom himself. In addition, he must constantly stoke fires under kettles without looking inside them. When he does peek, however, he discovers the military officers who had treated him poorly when he had been in the army. All the more reason for him to happily continue his work. When he leaves hell, the devil pays him gold but demands he remain loyal to him as "the devil's sooty brother," and the soldier obliges. In return the devil protects him from a swindling innkeeper, and eventually the soldier marries a princess and inherits a kingdom.

54   THE LETTUCE DONKEY
A huntsman helps a thirsty and starving hag and as a reward for his kindness, she instructs him on how to find a magical cloak and the heart of a bird that produces gold coins. Once he acquires the heart and the cloak, he sets out traveling and meets an old witch and her beautiful daughter. They trick the love-struck huntsman out of his treasures and leave him stranded on a distant mountain. He travels by cloud to a vegetable garden where he discovers a lettuce that can transform people into donkeys. He uses this magic on the witch and her daughter, who must work hard as donkeys for a miller. When the old witch dies, the huntsman rescues her repentant daughter, changes her back into a human, and marries her.

55   THE TURNIP

A poor farmer unwittingly grows a giant turnip, and decides to present it as a gift to the king. Impressed by its oddity, the king grants the farmer a good deal of land, livestock, and gold. When the farmer's wealthy brother hears of this, he takes his own gold and horses to the king, expecting a proportionate reward, but the king only gives him the giant turnip. Enraged, the brother seeks to vent his anger on his own brother. He hires murderers to lynch the turnip farmer, but the thugs are interrupted by a wandering scholar and they flee, leaving the farmer trapped in a sack hanging from a tree. The farmer convinces the scholar that it is in fact a "sack of wisdom" from which great secrets can be learned, and the scholar frees him, eager to exchange places. The turnip farmer rides away on the scholar's horse, and later sends someone to cut the fool down.

56   ONE-EYE, TWO-EYES, AND THREE-EYES

A girl with two eyes is persecuted as an abnormal freak by her mother and by her one-eyed and three-eyed sisters. One day Two-Eyes is visited by a wise woman who teaches her a secret spell: Ask the family goat for a table of food, and the food will magically appear. The two other sisters become suspicious, and Three-Eyes discovers the secret. Their mother kills the goat out of jealousy. Then the wise woman reappears and tells Two-Eyes to bury the goat's entrails, producing a tree with golden fruit that only Two-Eyes can pick. A young knight happens to pass by and witnesses this wonder. Two-Eyes explains her desperate situation to him and asks him to take her to his castle. Struck by her beauty, the prince agrees and eventually marries her.

57   THE WORN-OUT DANCING SHOES

A king proclaims that anyone who can explain why the dancing shoes of his twelve daughters are always worn to pieces will be allowed to marry one of them. But the secretive princesses trick one hopeful prince after another into drinking a sleeping potion. As a result, each and every prince who tries to discover the princesses' secret fails, and their heads are cut off. Finally, a poor but wise soldier outwits the princesses and, wearing an invisible cloak, follows them to a magical subterranean palace where they dance each night with handsome princes. Once he collects sufficient evidence to show to the king, he is allowed to wed the eldest daughter and is chosen to inherit the kingdom.

58   THE TWELVE HUNTSMEN

A prince chooses to fulfill the wish of his dying father by agreeing to marry another king's daughter, despite already being engaged to a princess. Deeply aggrieved, the princess finds eleven women similar to herself and together they dress as huntsmen and seek employment from her former fiancé, now a king. A wise talking lion in the court warns the king that the huntsmen are really women, and he decides to test them, but they are warned of this by a servant and remain undiscovered. But when the princess hears that the king is about to wed his new bride, she faints from grief and her engagement ring is revealed beneath her glove. The king finally recognizes his beloved. He then ignores his father's dying wish and marries his original bride.

59 IRON HANS

A king captures a dangerous wild man as brown as rusty iron from the bottom of a deep pool and imprisons him in a cage, forbidding anyone to release him on pain of death. But the wild man persuades the king's young son to set him free, and they both escape to the forest, where Iron Hans reveals that he has magical powers and declares that he will look after the young prince after they separate. Since the prince now has golden hair, he disguises himself and finds work in another kingdom as a gardener. Despite the disguise he attracts the attention of a princess, who falls in love with him. But the disguised prince wants to prove himself in war before he proposes to the princess, and, thanks to Iron Hans, he leads the king's army to victory. When the prince celebrates his victory with the princess and the king, Iron Hans appears and reveals that he is now released from a magic spell and gives all his treasures to the prince.

60 MOTHER HOLLE

A widow favors her own lazy daughter over her hardworking stepdaughter, whom she treats like a slave. One day the abused maiden accidentally drops a spinning reel down into a well and is forced to fetch it. After she jumps down the well, she loses consciousness and awakens in a beautiful meadow. As she wanders, she provides help to some baked bread and an apple tree. Finally, she meets the frightening but benevolent Mother Holle, who looks after her in exchange for regular housework. When the maiden decides to return home, Mother Holle sends her back covered with gold. This inspires the lazy stepsister to jump down the well to seek her own fortune, but she ignores the bread and apple tree and is too lazy to do Mother Holle's housework properly. She is sent home covered in a black pitch that can never be washed away.

61 THE GOOSE GIRL AT THE SPRING

While traveling about, a young count offers to help an old woman carry baskets of grass and fruit, only to find them incredibly heavy as the woman bullies him all the way to her mountain home. There he meets an ugly woman tending geese and is given a gift of a pearl for his help. Later the count meets a king and queen who recognize the pearl as a tear from their daughter, who had been banished from the kingdom for saying that she loved her father as much as salt. The king and queen suspect that their daughter is still alive, and they travel with the count to find her. When the count becomes separated from the king and queen, he discovers the goose girl removing her ugly skin at a spring, revealing the beautiful princess underneath. Soon thereafter the king, queen, and princess are reunited, and all is forgiven.

62 SIMELEI MOUNTAIN

A poor man secretly observes a band of robbers enter and exit a mountain by calling out a magical password, "Semsi Mountain." Once the man is alone, he tries it, and the cavern opens. It is filled with stolen riches, and the poor man takes home a modest amount to pay his debts. Meanwhile, his rich, greedy brother tricks him into revealing the secret of his new wealth and then travels to the mountain to plunder the cavern, but once inside he forgets the exact password and cannot open the cavern door. That evening the robbers return and cut off his head.

63   LAZY HEINZ

Lazy Heinz dreams of a life without work and finds a soul mate in the local maiden Fat Trina. They decide to trade their goats for a beehive because bees don't need to be herded, and they place their jug of honey on a high shelf in their bedroom. Since they are both terribly lazy, they keep a long stick next to their bed so they can protect their jug of honey from mice. However, due to their clumsiness the jug breaks and the honey flows all over the floor. Instead of getting upset, the pair welcome the opportunity to sleep in.

64   FITCHER'S BIRD

A sorcerer captures three sisters one at a time and takes them to his splendid house in a dark forest, where he allows them to go wherever they like except for one room which must never be opened. Curiosity overcomes them all: They discover dead people chopped to pieces. The sorcerer kills two of the sisters as punishment, but the third outwits him. She resurrects her siblings, tricks the sorcerer into taking them home, places an effigy of herself — a decorated skull — in the window, and escapes disguised as "Fitcher's bird" after covering herself in feathers. Her vengeful family later returns to lock the sorcerer in his house and burn it down.

65   STRONG HANS

A mother and her child named Hans are abducted by robbers and forced to live and work in a cave. The boy grows up big and strong, and one day he beats the robbers senseless with a fir-branch club before escaping with his mother and returning to their original home. His joyful father makes him a walking staff that weighs a hundred pounds, and Hans sets off traveling all about the world. Along his way he befriends two strong men and rescues a beautiful maiden from the clutches of a wicked dwarf. When his friends betray him, magical spirits come to his aid, enabling Hans to rescue the maiden a second time. Afterward he takes her home and marries her.

66   THE BLACKSMITH AND THE DEVIL

An impoverished blacksmith signs his soul away to the devil in exchange for ten years of wealth and happiness. When the devil comes to collect his soul, the blacksmith tricks him by asking him to turn himself into a mouse, whereupon the blacksmith sticks the devil into a magical sack and beats him until the contract is rescinded. Later, after a long and happy life, the blacksmith is turned away from heaven for having dealt with the devil. Then he is refused entry into hell for being a nuisance, but the devious blacksmith grabs two demons and nails them to the gates of hell. All this causes the devil to feel threatened, and he protests to the Lord until the blacksmith is finally admitted into heaven.

67   THE BLUE LIGHT

An injured soldier, discharged from duty by an ungracious king, is offered food and lodging by a witch. In return she asks him to retrieve a blue light from the bottom of a dry well, but abandons him there following an argument. The soldier ignites his pipe using the discovered light, thereby summoning a black dwarf who grants his every wish. The soldier asks that the witch be brought to account, and she is promptly put to death. He then seeks revenge on the king by kidnapping his daughter, but he is caught and sentenced to death. Allowed one final smoke of his pipe, he summons the dwarf, who beats the judges until the king gives the soldier his kingdom and his daughter for a wife.

68 THE NIXIE IN THE POND

In exchange for wealth, an impoverished miller promises a beautiful water nixie that he will give her the first creature born in his house. He thinks this will probably be a puppy or kitten; unfortunately it turns out to be his baby son. While still a boy, the son is warned to keep away from the pond, but when he becomes a man and marries, he ventures too close to the pond and is captured by the nixie. His devoted wife, intent on rescuing him, follows a dream, and on a distant mountain she asks a wise woman for help. Her advice enables the wife to help her husband escape from the pond. The enraged nixie turns herself into a tremendous wave and pursues husband and wife. They survive by temporarily transforming themselves into a frog and toad, but they become separated and lost in the flood. After years of sadness and longing, they meet accidentally while herding flocks of sheep and are happily reunited.

69 THE DOG AND THE SPARROW

An abused dog is befriended by a sparrow who promises to take care of him. When a mean and thoughtless wagoner runs over the dog with his wagon, the sparrow vows revenge. He breaks open the wagoner's wine barrels, pecks out the eyes of his horses, devours his wheat, and destroys his house. The sparrow doesn't relent until the wagoner is dead, struck by his own ax as he and his wife try to kill the bird in a mad panic.

70 THE WEDDING OF MRS. FOX

A fox with nine tails pretends to be dead in order to test his wife's fidelity. Soon after, a young fox arrives to court Mrs. Fox, but she rejects him because he only has one tail. A second fox appears with two tails, then a third with three, and so on. Each one is turned away until a young fox with nine tails appears, and, Mrs. Fox declares: "It's time to open the gate and the door, and sweep Mr. Fox out over the floor." But just as the wedding is being held, old Mr. Fox rises up in a rage and drives everyone, including Mrs. Fox, out of the house.

71 THE MASTER THIEF

A wealthy gentleman returns to his hometown and confesses to his old parents, who are peasants and do not recognize him, that he is a master thief. When the local lord hears about this, he challenges the young thief to accomplish three seemingly impossible tasks, or he will be sentenced to hang. With brilliant cunning the master thief steals a horse, a bedsheet, and a wedding ring from under the lord's nose. When challenged once more to steal a parson and a clerk from the church, the thief attaches lit candles to the backs of crabs and lets them loose in the graveyard at night. Convinced that the world is ending, the parson and clerk crawl into "Saint Peter's sack" seeking salvation, and are promptly delivered by the thief to the astounded lord, who banishes the thief from his land forever, and nobody ever hears from him again.

72   THE THIEF AND HIS MASTER

Tricked by a sexton into believing that his son's destiny is to become a thief, a father seeks to have his son trained by a master thief in a great forest. The master thief tells him that he will not have to pay anything if he can still recognize his son after one year of study. Fortunately, a dwarf reveals to him that his son will be disguised as a sparrow, and the father successfully avoids paying the disgruntled master. When the son later transforms himself into a horse as part of a scam, the disguised master thief purchases him and takes him home as a captive. However, the boy escapes, and a shapeshifting battle ensues until the master becomes a rooster and his former pupil, who has changed himself into a fox, bites off his head.

73   THE WATER OF LIFE

When a king falls terminally ill, his three sons embark on a dangerous journey to find the only cure, the legendary Water of Life. Along the way they meet a dwarf, but only the youngest prince is courteous enough to receive valuable instruction, while the arrogant older brothers are trapped in mountain passes. The young prince finds the water in a strange enchanted castle, frees a princess who urges him to return in one year, and helps three imperiled kingdoms on the way home. He also rescues his brothers, who replace the Water of Life with seawater that nearly kills the king. The youngest is blamed and sentenced to die, but a kind huntsman grants him his life. The brothers travel to the princess one by one, but only the youngest succeeds by ignoring a path of gold leading to the castle, and they are soon wed. Then she informs him that his father had learned about his innocence and pardoned him. They return to the king while his brothers flee before they can be punished.

74   THE MOON

In ancient times, four men discover a glowing ball — the moon — hanging like an oil lamp in an oak tree and claim it as their own. As each man ages and dies, a quarter of the moon is buried with him, until it eventually becomes whole again in the underworld. Freshly illuminated, the dead awake to cavort and fight. Indeed, they become so restless that Saint Peter must come to take the moon away and hang it in heaven.

75   THUMBLING

A poor farmer's wife gives birth to a clever little boy no bigger than a thumb. Although tiny, Thumbling enjoys many adventures — driving horses by sitting in their ears, thwarting thieves, and outwitting opportunistic men. After he is accidentally swallowed by a cow and escapes, Thumbling is once again swallowed whole by a wolf, but he tricks the animal into carrying him home, where the farmer and his wife kill the wolf and free their beloved child.

FURTHER READING

The edited extracts for this book come from *The Complete Fairy Tales of the Brothers Grimm* translated, introduced, and annotated by Jack Zipes (Bantam, 1987) and this is recommended as a companion volume for those wishing to fully experience each tale.

Also by Zipes, *The Original Folk and Fairy Tales of the Brothers Grimm: The Complete First Edition* (Princeton University Press, 2014) offers an insight into the very first "raw" editions compiled by Jacob and Wilhelm Grimm in 1812 and 1815, prior to subsequent editing. *The Irresistible Fairy Tale: The Cultural and Social History of a Genre* (Princeton University Press, 2012) provides a fascinating account of the evolution of fairy tales and their persistence throughout the world.

Fairy Tales from the Brothers Grimm, by Philip Pullman (Viking, 2012), was the original inspiration for my sculptural work, after I was asked to illustrate the German translation *Grimms Märchen*, published by Aladin in 2013. Pullman's retelling of fifty classic Grimms' tales remains faithful to the original while adding his own compelling voice and insightful commentary.

A book that particularly captured my imagination while working on *The Singing Bones* was *The Harry Winrob Collection of Inuit Sculpture* (Winnipeg Art Gallery, 2008). My own work is a pale shadow of the powerful narrative sculptures surveyed in this catalog.

ACKNOWLEDGMENTS

I'm grateful to Jack Zipes for his enthusiastic contribution to this project, and to Philip Pullman, Klaus Humann, and Nina Horn for rekindling my interest in Grimms' fairy tales. Many thanks to Neil Gaiman and Merrilee Heifetz; Arthur Levine, Emily Clement, Phil Falco, Sheila Marie Everett, Elizabeth Krych, and Shannon Rice; Jodie Webster, Erica Wagner, Sophie Byrne, Sandra Nobes, Richard Gwatkin, Theresa Bray, Clare Keighery, and Hilary Reynolds; and to Nghiem Ta for all her good advice. Much appreciation as always to my wife, Inari Kiuru, for her support and very useful sculpting, photography, and design advice. And to Vida, for wanting a big skull on the cover.

ARTIST'S NOTE: All of the sculptures in this book are between 2¼ inches and 16 inches tall, primarily made of papier-mâché, air-drying clay (DAS), and paint, photographed and digitally edited by the artist. Other sculptural materials used include aluminum foil, wax, wood, iron and bronze patina, gold leaf, wire, paper, string, fabric, sand, sugar and salt (for watery ripples), pepper, rice, dragées, nails, sticks, rocks, berries, blossoms, and leaves. For more about the making of this book, visit www.shauntan.net.

Library of Congress Cataloging-in-Publication Data

Names: Tan, Shaun, adapter, illustrator. | Gaiman, Neil, author of foreword.
| Zipes, Jack, 1937– author of introduction, translator. | Grimm, Jacob,
1785–1863. | Grimm, Wilhelm, 1786–1859.
Title: The singing bones : inspired by Grimms' fairy tales / Shaun Tan ;
foreword by Neil Gaiman ; introduced by Jack Zipes.
Description: First American edition. | New York, NY : Arthur A. Levine Books,
an imprint of Scholastic Inc., 2016. | "Text abridged and adapted from
translations of Grimms' fairy tales, © Jack Zipes." | Summary: Selection
and adaptation of seventy-five Grimms' fairy tales, as translated by Jack
Zipes, and newly illustrated by Shaun Tan. | Includes bibliographical references and index.
Identifiers: LCCN 2016014031 | ISBN 9780545946124 (hardcover : alk. paper)
Subjects: LCSH: Kinder- und Hausmärchen—Adaptations. | Fairy tales—Germany. | Folklore—
Germany—Juvenile literature. | CYAC: Fairy tales. | Folklore—Germany.
Classification: LCC PZ8.T168 Si 2016 | DDC 398.21/0943 [E] —dc23
LC record available at https://lccn.loc.gov/2016014031

10 9 8 7 6 5 4 3 2 1   16 17 18 19 20

Printed in China   62
First American edition, October 2016

Book design by Shaun Tan, Sandra Nobes, and Phil Falco